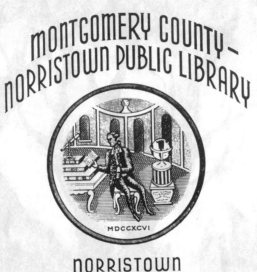

The Never-Ending Greenness

Neil Waldman

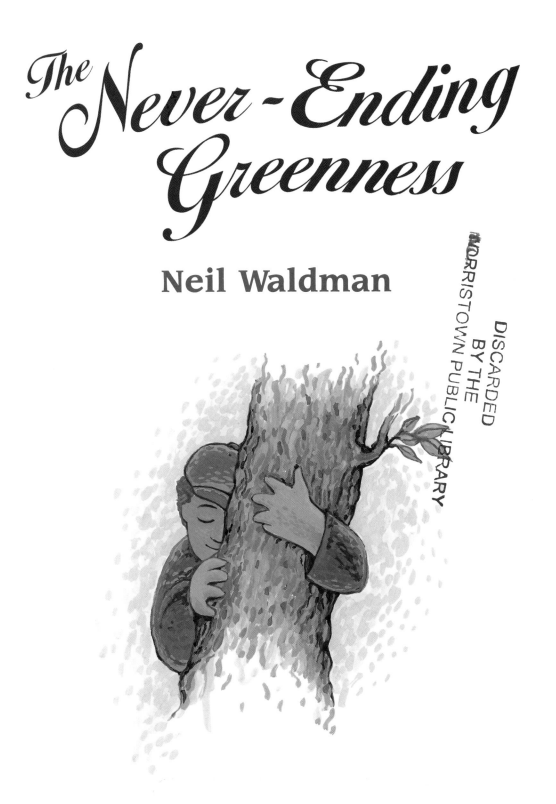

MORROW JUNIOR BOOKS

NEW YORK

Acrylics were used for the full-color illustrations.
The text type is 14-point Leawood Book.

Copyright © 1997 by Neil Waldman

Printed in Hong Kong by South China Printing Company (1988) Ltd.

1 2 3 4 5 6 7 8 9 10

Library of Congress Cataloging-in-Publication Data
Waldman, Neil.
The never-ending greenness/Neil Waldman.
p. cm.
Summary: When his family comes to live in Israel after the end
of World War II, a young boy begins planting and caring for trees,
a practice that spreads across the whole country.
ISBN 0-688-14479-9 (trade)—ISBN 0-688-14480-2 (library)
[1. Trees—Fiction.   2. Jews—Fiction.   3. Israel—Fiction.]
I. Title. PZ7.W146Ne 1997 [E]—dc20 96-14844 CIP AC

For Brucie, my loving brother, who has walked
with me many times through the forests of Judea

Historical Note

When the Jewish people returned to Israel after an absence of
nearly two thousand years, they found the land barren and empty.
Individually and in groups, the settlers soon began planting trees.
Under the leadership of the Jewish National Fund, more than two
hundred and twenty million trees have been planted since the turn
of the century. Jews around the world honor this heritage with a yearly
tree-planting celebration called Tu b'Shvat (too bish-VHAT). The name
of the holiday comes from the day it is held: the fifteenth day of the
Hebrew month of Shvat.

The Vilna Ghetto was erected by the Nazis in Lithuania during the
Second World War. Some Jews escaped by climbing over the ghetto
wall and hiding in the surrounding forests. Those who remained were
taken to a place called Ponar and executed by firing squad. Some of
those who escaped, and survived, were held in detention camps
before emigrating to eretz Yisrael (EHR-etz yis-rah-EL), the land of
Israel, where they joined in the bitter struggle for the survival of the
newborn Jewish state.

I was born many years ago in a city called Vilna. I remember my papa's bakery, all filled with wonderful smells. I remember the synagogue and the great library. But mostly I remember the trees. Green in summer, bare in winter, they lined the streets like friendly old men, stretching their arms toward the sun-filled skies. I remember the miracle of early spring, their branches slowly filling with buds, then tiny yellowish feathers, and finally full green leaves.

But then the war came. Soldiers marched into our neighborhood. They told us we had to leave our homes and forced us into a place called the ghetto. Papa found us a small room in the corner of a crowded, dark apartment. We soon grew hungry and spent our days searching for food. After a while, we even began looking in garbage cans.

That spring, there was no green anywhere. As strange as it may seem to you, the people had eaten all the grass, and even the weeds. What remained was a world of stone and mud, crisscrossed by brown-puddled streets where skinny, puffy-eyed people drifted like ghosts.

Papa told us we had to try to escape. Late one night we tiptoed down the back alleyways and climbed over the ghetto wall. We ran and ran to the forest outside Vilna, and as I lay hidden beneath the branches of an ancient oak, I began to cry. "Please protect us," I whispered, looking up at the sheltering leaves.

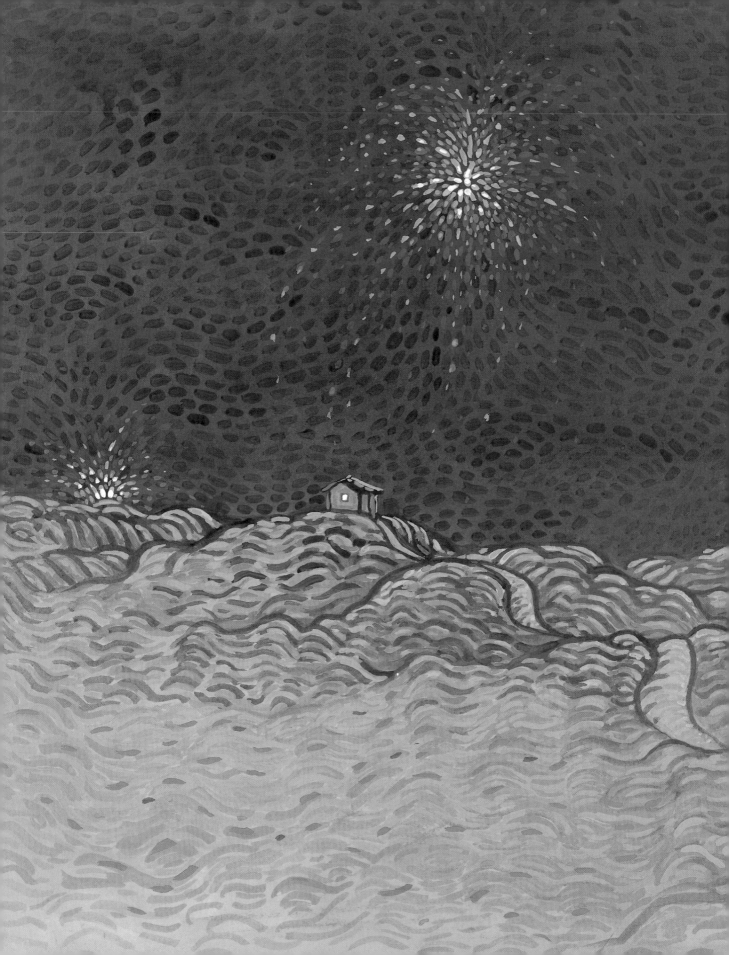

In the weeks and months that followed, we crept from hiding place to hiding place until finally the war ended. We boarded a large ship crammed full of people and sailed to our new home in a place called eretz Yisrael. We were given a little wooden house on a dusty hill, where we would start our new lives. But there was war here too. Papa was forced to join the army, and Mama and I were left at home by ourselves. We often heard the explosion of guns in the distance. At night the sky would flicker with bursting bombs that we called lightning. I usually slept in Mama's bed.

Mama and I spent many days hiking through the hills and valleys around our village. We discovered some amazing places: a crusader's castle, where we journeyed by candlelight through a secret passageway beneath the stone floor; a hidden spring of icy water, where we watched silently as six gazelles came to drink; and an ancient city of caves carved into a hillside, where we found some pieces of broken pottery and a Roman coin.

Then one spring morning we came upon a newborn tree growing out from between some rocks. "Look at this," Mama said, touching the shiny leaves. "It's a shame these little trees rarely survive the summer."

"Let's dig it up and save its life," I insisted.

And so we did. We planted it outside my bedroom window and gave it a thorough soaking. Each morning, I would run to my window to make sure that my little tree was still there. And every evening I would slowly pour a glass of water over it, helping it to survive the dry season.

In the fall, when the rains began, my tree was still alive. And in the springtime three new branches appeared, filled with tiny sparkling leaves.

I smiled every time I looked at my tree. It was already twice as big as it was when I planted it.

Then one night I had a dream. Our house was surrounded by a forest of swaying trees. As I stood at my window, two golden birds swooped down from the sky and carried me back up with them. As far as I could see in every direction, the earth was covered with a thick forest carpet. Then the birds began humming a beautiful melody, and the clouds, the wind, and the trees joined in. Like a thousand gentle flutes, they filled the air with vibrations of wonder. I broke free from the golden birds and soared high above them, like an eagle.

I awoke with my heart pounding. I jumped into my clothes and raced out into the empty hills. I walked that entire day, searching among the rocks and crevices until finally I came upon another seedling, growing high on a rocky hillside. I carefully dug it up and brought it home, planting it next to my first little tree.

I went out again the next day, and the day after that and the day after that. By spring's end there was a grove of thirty-two trees in front of our house. And when the rains began to fall in October, twenty-four of them were still alive.

I knew I was making my dream come true. When grown-ups asked me about my trees, I told them about the magical forest in my dream and they smiled. They didn't take me seriously, but it didn't matter. I knew that someday all the hills really would be green.

Then, on a wonderful day, Papa came home. He soon found work in the village bakery and joined us in our new life.

One Saturday morning, as Papa and I stood admiring my beautiful grove, I told him about my dream. Papa smiled, but not like the others. *His* smile made me feel proud.

"You know," he began, "you're helping to return these hills to the way they were thousands of years ago, when forests covered our land. But many wars have been fought here. And many conquerors have stolen from the land. They cut down the forests to build fortresses and railroads until almost all the trees were gone. Over the centuries, winter rains washed away the topsoil. With no trees and no shade, the days grew hotter and drier, and many of the animals began to disappear. Now it looks almost like a desert."

"Things are going to change," I whispered.

As the years passed I continued planting. My grove of trees crept slowly up the hillside, and the little tree beneath my window was now higher than the roof. In the spring, migrating storks rested in the branches. And on summer afternoons Mama, Papa, and I sat in the cool shade in front of our house, the breeze drying the sweat from our foreheads.

When I graduated from high school, I began working at the bakery with Papa. On evenings and weekends I continued planting. Several friends joined me, and we began cultivating other groves in the surrounding hills. Then I began to hear that people all over the country were doing the same thing.

For the past fifty years we have been planting trees. And every year, to celebrate a holiday called Tu b'Shvat, children from all over the world send us thousands of seedlings to plant. Each year, the forest spreads, covering our country with a carpet of green.

The land is changing. There are more birds every year. The streams don't dry up so quickly, and beds of mushrooms have begun to grow in the darkness of the forest floor. Like a miracle from the Torah, a generation of newborn trees is springing up from the fallen seeds of those we planted years ago.

And someday, perhaps, two golden birds will return to carry me high above the hills, so I can peer out across the never-ending greenness and hear the song of a thousand gentle flutes.